Fire in the Forest

A Cycle of Growth and Renewal

by
LAURENCE
PRINGLE

paintings by
BOB MARSTALL

ATHENEUM BOOKS FOR YOUNG READERS

This book would not have been possible without Don Despain, research biologist at the Greater Yellowstone Field Station of the National Biological Survey. His comments on fire ecology in such magazines as the *New Yorker* were a major inspiration for the book. Once the book was underway, I benefited greatly from his generous contributions of encouragement, time, and expertise. During my research visit to Yellowstone, Mr. Despain suggested sites to visit, discussed fire and forest ecology, and answered many questions. His book, *Yellowstone Vegetation,* was an invaluable resource, and he loaned photographs to me for use back in the studio. As the book neared completion, he reviewed the text for scientific accuracy.

I wish to thank Matthew Kelty, assistant professor of forestry, University of Massachusetts at Amherst, for his assistance and advice; Michael Linde of the National Park Service for his professional advice and personal encouragement; and the National Park Service staff at Yellowstone.

And special thanks to Harold Underdown, my editor, who followed through on his original vision for this book.

—BOB MARSTALL

DEDICATED TO LOIS—PASSIONATE, VITAL, CARING, AND SORELY MISSED

—L. P.

IN MEMORY OF MY MOTHER, ETHEL MARSTALL, AND MY WIFE, DENISE CALLAGHAN, FOR THEIR LOVE AND SUPPORT THROUGHOUT MY WORK ON THE PAINTINGS FOR THIS BOOK.

—B. M.

ATHENEUM BOOKS FOR YOUNG READERS, an imprint of Simon & Schuster Children's Publishing Division, 1230 Avenue of the Americas, New York, New York 10020. Text copyright © 1995 by Laurence Pringle. Illustrations copyright © 1995 by Bob Marstall. All rights reserved including the right of reproduction in whole or in part in any form. The text for this book is set in Meridien. The illustrations are rendered in oil paint. Manufactured in the United States of America. First edition.   10   9   8   7   6   5   4   3   2   1

Library of Congress Cataloging-in-Publication Data. Pringle, Laurence P. Fire in the forest : a cycle of growth and renewal / by Laurence Pringle ; paintings by Bob Marstall. — 1st ed.   p.   cm.
Includes bibliographical references. ISBN 0-689-80394-X   1. Fire ecology—Juvenile literature.   2. Forest fires—Juvenile literature.   3. Forest ecology—Juvenile literature.   4. Fire ecology—Yellowstone National Park—Juvenile literature.   5. Forest fires—Yellowstone National Park—Juvenile literature.   6. Forest ecology—Yellowstone National Park—Juvenile literature.   7. Lodgepole pine—Yellowstone National Park—Ecology—Juvenile literature. 8. Yellowstone National Park—Juvenile literature. I. Marstall, Bob. II. Title. QH545.F5P73 1995 574.5′2642—dc20   92-32257

Overleaf:
MOUNTAIN BLUEBIRD
(about 7 in. long)

AS NATURAL AS RAIN

For as long as humans have lived, fire has been both friend and foe. As we sit by a campfire or fireplace and gaze into the glowing coals, fire gives warmth, contentment, a kind of magic. In an instant, though, it can bring pain, loss, terror.

Fire running wild in nature can be a great destroyer of houses in its path. In California's chaparral brushlands it has burned whole neighborhoods to the ground. In 1987 a wildfire in northeast China destroyed more than ten thousand homes. And in the summer of 1988, hundreds of fires struck western North America. Years of drought in the West had created conditions that produced the worst fire season in American history. Forests burned in Oregon, Washington, and Texas. More than two million acres blazed in Alaska. And eight huge fires swept through more than a third of Yellowstone National Park in Wyoming, Montana, and Idaho.

Friend or foe? To many politicians, news reporters, and ordinary citizens, all wildfire is bad, and the Yellowstone fires were a catastrophe. In addition to burning wilderness forest and threatening visitor centers within the national park, flames threatened homes and marketable timber outside park boundaries. More than nine thousand firefighters struggled to quell the fires.

No one questions the great effort to save park buildings and private property.

ELK
(4–5 ft. high at shoulder)

Overleaf: THE FOREST, 300 to 350 YEARS AFTER THE PREVIOUS FIRE

For the great wilderness park, however, the fires were no catastrophe, but a rare yet predictable natural event. Similar large fires raged through forests there around the year 1700. Two or three centuries from now, vast areas of the Yellowstone region will probably burn again.

To ecologists, fire is a normal and even welcome force in nature. Ever since there has been vegetation dry enough to be lit by lightning, fire has been part of earth's environment. For millions of years, fire has been as natural as rain in forests, prairies, and many other habitats.

From the Pine Barrens of New Jersey to the Everglades of Florida, plant and animal communities have evolved with wildfire. They thrive under its influence. Fire brings change, diversity, and new life. The Yellowstone fires of 1988 were no exception.

A MOSAIC OF LIFE

The paintings in this book show a landscape of the northern Rocky Mountains. You might see a similar view along a road within the 2.2 million acres of Yellowstone National Park. You might also see it far from the park, for the vast Greater Yellowstone ecosystem covers twelve million acres in the northern Rockies.

The Yellowstone ecosystem is a mosaic of life. From lookout points you can see a patchwork of meadows, stream valleys, rocky ridges and peaks, and forests of different types, both young and old. The pattern is a puzzle: Why are trees and other vegetation arranged that way? Why isn't the entire landscape covered with one kind of forest?

Part of the answer lies in the distribution of the rocks and soils of Yellowstone. These cause some plants to thrive in certain areas and not in others. Meadows are found where the soils are high in calcium and other minerals,

MATURE LODGEPOLE PINE

forests where minerals are less plentiful. Lodgepole pine, in particular, can grow in thin soils that are poor in minerals. Small differences in climate also affect where plants live. Engelmann spruce does best on northern and eastern slopes, which have a cooler climate than southern and western slopes.

Fire, too, plays a part in creating the mosaic of life in the Yellowstone region. Since no timber cutting is allowed within the national park, a young forest growing right alongside an old forest marks the border of a past fire. A new generation of trees rises where wildfire burned part of a stand of mature trees.

Throughout the region, when ecologists dig in the soil, they find layers of charcoal—evidence of fires that burned centuries ago. Fire scars on trees also reveal when their trunks were burned in the past. The trees did not die; they kept growing. They continued to form annual rings of wood which can be counted, giving a tally of the years since the fire occurred. From evidence like this, ecologists have learned about the fire history of the Yellowstone ecosystem, and especially of Yellowstone's most widespread trees, lodgepole pines.

Native Americans used young trunks of the trees to support their lodges, so they were given the name lodgepole pines. Some 80 percent of Yellowstone's trees are lodgepole pines, and you'll see mostly this species in the illustrations.

Large wildfires are uncommon in young lodgepole pine forests. As a lodgepole pine forest grows older, however, it becomes more vulnerable to fire. Towering pines—often more than two centuries old—finally die and fall to the earth. Their trunks and limbs, which decay slowly, make potential fuel for a forest fire.

The fall of each giant creates a sunny opening, where young trees grow quickly. They include a new generation of lodgepole pines, but also subalpine fir and Engelmann spruce, whose limbs reach close to the ground. These branches are also potential fuel, and can serve as ladders for a fire burning along the forest floor. They enable flames to leap upward into the crowns of the firs and spruces, then into the crowns of lodgepole pines.

In 1988, about a third of Yellowstone's lodgepole pine forests were between 250 and 350 years old. They were at their most burnable stage, vulnerable to a major fire. Such fires are rare, but in 1988 nature provided a key ingredient in the

weather. It was unusually windy and dry; in fact, it was the driest summer in 112 years of weather record keeping at Yellowstone National Park.

Fire ecologists sometimes measure the water content of potential fuels—grasses, small branches, dead trees—in order to estimate the likelihood of forest fires. They have found that few fires start if the moisture content of plants is greater than 16 percent. Those that do soon die out. If fuels hold between 12 and 16 percent water, some fires may burn two hundred to three hundred acres. At 8 to 12 percent moisture, fires start readily and burn freely.

By late July 1988, the moisture found in dead trees in the Yellowstone area was just 7 percent, and reached levels as low as 2 or 3 percent in grasses and twigs. After nearly three centuries, the stage was set for major forest fires in the Yellowstone ecosystem.

FOREST FIRE!

Many forest fires are started by people, mostly by accident. Of the eight major fires that burned in Yellowstone National Park in 1988, three were started by people, all of them beginning outside the park.

Lightning also starts forest fires. Each day an estimated half-million lightning bolts strike forests on earth. Only a tiny fraction cause fires. In the Yellowstone ecosystem, a fire is most likely to start if lightning strikes an old spruce or fir tree that has a plentiful growth of lichens on its limbs and bark. Dry lichens are quick to burn. If the treetop catches fire, flaming twigs and other firebrands fall to the forest floor. When a firebrand lands among dry leaves and other fuels, a wildfire begins. Most lightning-caused fires burn a small area and go out.

Every year nature demonstrates, in different kinds of forests and also in other habitats, that it is usually difficult to start a large wildfire. Conditions must be just right. Anyone who has tried to start a campfire knows that it is vital to have

FIREWEED
(detail)

enough dry fuel at hand. And success sometimes depends on giving the fire more oxygen; you blow air on glowing embers so that they will burst into flame. Major wildfires must also have plenty of dry fuel, and wind can play a key role, nurturing a fire and speeding it along.

Large fires, in fact, create their own weather. Hot air rises far above the flames, and this causes cooler air to rush in near ground level. The result can even be a firestorm—the most spectacular of all wildfires. A firestorm seems like a roaring beast with a mind of its own. It may change direction, or pause and then race swiftly forward.

Many people picture all forest fires as raging firestorms, but such fires are rare. Each wildfire is unique. Each has a life: It is born, lives for a short or long time, then dies. Some fires smolder undetected for long periods, even over winter, then revive when burning conditions improve.

Wildfires often have a daily rhythm. They usually slow at night, when air temperatures cool and winds die down. The 1988 Yellowstone fires were unusual because at night, winds often kept blowing, and temperatures remained high. The fires kept moving, offering firefighters little rest. In the end, the efforts of firefighters saved many buildings in the Yellowstone region, but failed to completely halt any fires. A quarter inch of rain did that.

Most wildfires creep along the ground, consuming the dead leaves, twigs, and other natural litter that lie there. If flames leap into the forest canopy, the crown fire may race ahead of the surface fire from which it arose. Trees become giant torches, with flames reaching two hundred feet into the air.

Updrafts lift burning embers into the sky. They may land a mile or more ahead of the main blaze, starting new fires. Embers carried by the wind cross roads, rivers, and other barriers that might ordinarily bring a fire to a halt. In Yellowstone National Park, flying embers enabled fire to leap the Grand Canyon of the Yellowstone River.

The life of a wildfire is seldom simple. As it moves, it meets new terrain and conditions that change its behavior—and its effects on the environment.

Here, in an area littered with fallen trees and large amounts of pine needles, twigs, and other fuels, the fire burns with intense heat for several hours. It kills

THIRTEEN-LINED GROUND SQUIRREL
(7–12 in. long, excluding tail)

Overleaf: A FEW DAYS AFTER THE FIRE

MOUNTAIN PINE BEETLE
(actual size: about 1/5 in. long)

LODGEPOLE PINE AFTER FIRE

seeds and insects in the top few inches of soil. Over there, however, the fire finds much less fuel and moves briskly over the surface. Its heat barely penetrates the soil. Along one edge of the fire, flames reach a stand of young pine trees. There is so little fuel on the ground that the fire can no longer advance in that direction. The young forest is spared.

At the leading edge of the fire, flames climb the dry bark of a leaning dead tree and ignite the needles of an Engelmann spruce. Fire leaps to the lodgepole pine canopy. A spectacular crown fire blazes for a distance, but stops when it reaches pine trees that have been killed by mountain pine beetles (the larvae of these beetles feed within lodgepole pine trunks and often kill them). The trees have lost their needles and provide little fuel for the crown fire.

The wildfire's brief life comes to an end. A day or two later, you would be able to walk over the area it burned. You would see for yourself whether the fire had "consumed" or "destroyed" the forest, as reporters and television news-readers often say. You would probably find that the fire had killed many trees but only damaged others. It skipped some areas entirely.

The major 1988 fires of the Yellowstone region acted like this, for all their intensity. They left behind a pattern of burned, partly burned, and unburned habitats. They created a new mosaic of life.

AFTERMATH

Wildfires do not, as many people fear, leave behind a landscape littered with dead animals. The fires usually move slowly. Large animals just get out of the way. Even snakes have time to flee, and burrowing animals are usually not harmed as the fire passes overhead.

The 1988 Yellowstone fires were unusually fierce and fast moving. Some days they advanced ten miles. Nevertheless, they killed few large wild animals.

After the fires died, park biologists searched for animal carcasses where the danger to wildlife had been greatest—in areas where high winds had pushed flames rapidly along a broad front. They found about 250 dead elk, a tiny fraction of the park's population. The elk had died of smoke inhalation, not from heat or flame. Small numbers of bison, deer, moose, and black bears also perished.

Elk and bison grazed calmly in meadows while the forest fires raged nearby. Along the edges of fires, coyotes hunted for fleeing rodents. So did many predatory birds, including eagles, kestrels, falcons, hawks, and even great gray owls. One biologist saw about forty ferruginous hawks hunting in one area of the national park. This species is uncommon in the park. It usually catches mice and ground squirrels on prairies. Columns of smoke rising thousands of feet in the air may have attracted the hawks from afar.

FERRUGINOUS HAWK
(wingspread about 2 ft.)

This behavior of predatory birds has also been observed near wildfires in prairies, the Everglades, and other habitats. In Africa, eagles and other meat-eating birds are attracted to wildfires. They catch lizards and rodents that are flushed from hiding places by advancing flames.

The patchwork pattern left by a forest fire usually includes some grim landscapes studded with blackened tree skeletons. The ground is strewn with ashes. This death scene is brief, and deceptive.

Wildfires have been called nature's great recyclers. In a sense, all living things borrow a supply of the earth's minerals for a while. Wildfire makes the pine needles, branches, and other once-living things of the forest give them back. They become available to other life.

Ashes from forest fires, sometimes five inches deep, are rich with calcium, phosphorus, and other minerals. These nutrients support an explosion of new plant growth. Seeds in the soil that were unharmed spring to life. In the Yellowstone ecosystem, the burned land was soon covered with grasses, fireweed, Ross's sedge, aster, western meadow rue, and grouse whortleberry.

When fire burns the green crowns of lodgepole pines, firs, and spruces, the trees die, but most shrubs and other woody forest plants survive. Their old stems are charred and dead, but new stems sprout from roots and rhizomes. Aspens, in particular, recover quickly from wildfires.

Overleaf: TWO TO FOUR YEARS AFTER THE FIRE

A COYOTE POUNCING
(3 ft., excluding tail)

Although aspens reproduce from seeds, once established, they spread from extensive root systems. In the Yellowstone ecosystem, according to park biologist Don Despain, some aspens grow from root systems that may have originated thousands of years ago. Then they were food for browsing mammals that died out in North America: mammoths, horses, and camels. Now elk browse on the recent growth of these ancient plants. When fire kills their aboveground parts, the aspens send up a dense stand of woody sprouts. In their first year, these little trees may grow three to six feet.

FIRE SPECIES

Every summer there is news about large forest fires in the West. Such fires are rare in the Midwest and East, where rainfall is abundant. Moisture keeps fires from starting. It also helps speed the process of decay, so fallen leaves and other potential fire fuels do not build up on the forest floor. When fires do occur, they tend to creep along, and rarely reach the crowns of trees.

In the arid West, fallen leaves and other fuels decay slowly and accumulate over the years. Also, the very dryness of the climate invites wildfires. As a result, western forests are home to many plants called fire species. They are specially adapted to survive the fires that have long been part of their environment. In fact, fire helps some of these plants to reproduce.

Aspen is one fire species. Like aspen, many Western shrubs send up new stems after a fire. They include redstem, wedgeleaf, snowbrush, and deerbrush. The plant community known as chaparral, which grows in southern California and northern Mexico, includes several kinds of shrubs and small trees that are fire species. They sprout profusely after a fire, and the fire itself stimulates their seeds to sprout.

The grass that grows beneath Douglas fir forests in the West is another fire species. Pine grass almost never flowers until it is burned. Then new growth sprouts and these stems produce a bounty of flowers and seeds.

Lodgepole pine, jack pine, and several other evergreen trees are fire species, too. Fire can play a key role in their reproduction by causing their cones to release seeds.

Lodgepole pines often produce two kinds of seed-bearing cones—some that open and release seeds under normal conditions, and some that depend on a fire's heat to free their seeds. These are called serotinous (which means "closed") cones. They are hard as rocks, their scales sealed shut with sticky resins.

In the Yellowstone ecosystem, each serotinous cone contains between ten and twenty-four seeds. The seeds remain viable for years, and the cones accumulate for decades on lodgepole pine branches. They represent a reserve of many thousands, perhaps millions, of seeds per acre.

Instead of saving for a rainy day, lodgepole pines save the seeds for a fiery one. Temperatures between 113 and 140 degrees Fahrenheit melt the cones' resins, allow scales to open, and free the seeds. Some are killed by fire, but many fall onto a forest floor newly rich with minerals and newly open to full sunlight— ideal conditions for lodgepole pine seedlings.

Squirrels, deer mice, and other seed eaters consume many pine seeds, but plenty remain to sprout during the spring following a wildfire. At three years of age, the seedlings number more than a thousand an acre, but they are less than eight inches tall. For a few years immediately after a wildfire, the young pines are scarcely visible. Fireweed, grasses, and other plants form a dense cover over a landscape that is punctuated by tree skeletons, both fallen and standing. Nevertheless, the pines eventually rise above the other plants and begin to dominate the landscape. At ten years of age, they usually stand five feet tall.

Having all started growth at the same time, the pines are known as an even-aged stand. As they grow larger and compete for light and water, the number of trees on an acre dwindles. Of the original thousand seedlings on an acre, after two centuries perhaps only two hundred to three hundred trees remain. The survivors are still an even-aged stand, born together and likely to die together in

A SEROTINOUS LODGEPOLE PINECONE
before and after fire
(1–2 in. high)

LODGEPOLE PINE SEEDS

A LODGEPOLE PINE SEEDLING
(2–4 in. high)

Overleaf: TWENTY TO THIRTY YEARS AFTER THE FIRE

the next great forest fire. Their serotinous cones, packed with seeds, hang ready on their branches.

E B B   A N D   F L O W

Immediately after the great fires of 1988 in Yellowstone National Park, biologists looked for elk and other large animals killed by fire. They discovered that others had beaten them to it. The carcasses were being fed upon by ravens, magpies, bald eagles, coyotes, and both grizzly and black bears.

These scavengers were only the first of many organisms to benefit from the wildfires. But *benefit* can be a misleading term. It suggests that the Yellowstone ecosystem—or any wild habitat—is made up of winners and losers. Ecologists prefer to say that change is inevitable in nature and that it affects different organisms in different ways.

Fireweed flourished for a few years after the Yellowstone fires, then gradually became scarce. Sometime in the future it will grow bountifully again. The populations of other organisms also ebb and flow as a result of the ecological processes at work in the wild Yellowstone area.

The wildfires had both short- and long-term effects. For a few years they

BLACK-BILLED MAGPIE
(17–22 in. long)

caused a rise in the numbers of deer mice, which eat seeds, and a drop in the numbers of redbacked voles, rodents that eat mushrooms. By burning many stands of mature lodgepole pines, fires also reduced the favored habitat of the boreal owl, sage thrasher, and ruby-crowned kinglet. Yellowstone's populations of these birds have declined. They will rise again when new forests mature—many years in the future.

DEER MOUSE
(3–4 in., excluding tail)

Thousands of charred lodgepole pines and other dead trees now lie on the ground or still stand. A dead tree can be a lively place, a home and food source for fungi, ants, beetles, and many other organisms. In turn, both black and grizzly bears will find food in the logs, ripping into them and feasting on beetle and ant larvae.

Standing dead trees—called snags—offer home sites for birds that nest in holes. Woodpeckers chip out cavities and usually nest in them just once. Then the cavities are nest sites for tree swallows and mountain bluebirds, both insect-eating species that thrive in the sunny openings left by forest fires.

REDBACKED VOLE
(3½–4½ in., excluding tail)

After a fire in the Yellowstone region, populations of these birds rise sharply. Then the new, young forest grows taller. One by one, the dead trees fall over. The number of tree swallows and mountain bluebirds decline. Like fireweed, these species will rise again after another fire.

Park biologists carefully noted any changes in the populations of elk and other large mammals, including grizzly bears, an endangered species. The fires killed just two grizzlies out of a population of two hundred or more. They did kill many whitebark pine trees, the source of pine nuts that are an important autumn food for grizzly bears. The bears seemed to turn to other foods. In the spring, emerging hungry from hibernation, grizzlies were able to feed on numerous dead elk that did not survive the winter.

The Yellowstone region's elk population had been at a high point before the 1988 fires, with a summer population of about 31,000 elk in the national park itself. Mild winters had made more food available during those critical cold months. Few elk had died.

The fires burned parts of the elk's summer and winter range, and the winter that followed was the first in several years with normal snowfall and deep cold.

Overleaf: SEVENTY TO EIGHTY YEARS AFTER THE FIRE

By springtime, several thousand elk had died. Many others survived and faced a brighter future as shrubs, and other forage plants responded to increased sunlight and plentiful nutrients in ashes.

Overall, wherever fire had touched the Yellowstone landscape, it brought an increased diversity of plant and animal life.

FIRE CYCLES

After the last charred snag tumbles to the ground, there is little sign of the crown fire that swept through a lodgepole pine forest a few decades earlier. Trees of the new generation compete fiercely for soil nutrients, sunlight, and water. Weaker trees die. So do most of the shrubs and other forest-floor plants that had thrived just after the fire. They dwindle away once the pine limbs overhead form a canopy that blocks most of the sunlight. The variety of plants in the forest is reduced, and so is the variety of insects, birds, and other life.

Young lodgepole pine forests are sometimes so densely packed that they are called "doghair" thickets or forests. These forests have so little fuel that fires rarely start in them. They are also natural firebreaks. Large fires usually sputter to a stop at the edge of these forests, or go around them. The forest floor is almost bare of living plants. A few decaying logs remain, the remains of trees that fell during the thinning process, or fallen snags from the long-ago fire that helped create this forest. The main fuel is the forest canopy itself, and a ground fire has no way to reach it.

Sometime after 150 years, the lodgepole pine forest begins to change, and the changes make it more and more vulnerable to fire. Some trees die, creating sunny patches on the forest floor. Wildflowers and shrubs begin to grow there, along with some lodgepole pine seedlings, which thrive in sunny openings. Engelmann spruce and subalpine fir begin to grow in the shade of the pine

LODGEPOLE PINE SAPLING

canopy; their seedlings do well there. They form an understory of seedlings and saplings.

Changes continue, and by the time the forest is three hundred years old, the lodgepole pine canopy is quite broken. The spruce and fir trees have grown as tall as the remaining lodgepole pines. Many fallen pines lie on the forest floor, their trunks sometimes crisscrossed. This is a difficult forest to walk through, but it has a greater diversity of life than earlier stages.

Given another century, this forest would continue to change. All of the

QUAKING ASPEN
20–60 ft.

LODGEPOLE PINE
75–80 ft.

SUBALPINE FIR
40–100 ft.

ENGELMANN SPRUCE
100–125 ft.

Overleaf: 180 TO 220 YEARS AFTER THE FIRE

original lodgepole pines would die. There would be no replacements, since pine seedlings could not survive in the shade from a new canopy of large spruce and fir. This Engelmann spruce–subalpine fir forest could go on indefinitely. It would be the climax forest, the final stage, on many lands of the Yellowstone ecosystem.

This climax stage is uncommon, since fire usually prevents it from being reached. The abundant fuel in an old lodgepole pine forest invites fire, and lightning often provides the spark. Then the cycle of life starts all over again.

In the Yellowstone ecosystem, fire is the force that makes lodgepole pine and not spruce and fir the most abundant type of forest. Fire plays the same key role in other ecosystems, too. In large parts of southeastern New Jersey, the climax forest is oak, but periodic fires prevent oaks from reaching maturity. The fires maintain the famous Pinelands or Pine Barrens of New Jersey, in which pitch pine and scrub pine thrive. They are fire species, whose seed cones are opened by a fire's heat.

In the Southeast, fire keeps pine forests from being replaced by oaks and other hardwoods. And in the West, periodic fires help maintain the open, parklike quality of ponderosa pine forests. Without fire, ponderosa pine is replaced by dense stands of white fir and Douglas fir.

In forests and other habitats around the world, fire continues to exert its ancient power to affect plant-animal communities.

BEYOND *BAMBI* AND SMOKEY

In 1992, severe drought in the Northwest led to many large fires. They covered more than a million acres. And, according to the news media, the fires "destroyed" or "devastated" the woods. At the same time, reporting on changes in the Yellowstone area since the great fires there, the news media hailed its "recovery" or "rebirth."

Ecologists are disappointed by this misunderstanding of wildfire. People today seem to know less about fire than the people who lived in North America thousands of years ago. Wherever they lived, on prairies or forests, Native Americans sometimes set fires. They knew that the deer and other animals they hunted, and the plants they gathered for food, did well after the land was burned.

Many people today seem to feel that any out-of-control fire is bad. For some, this attitude began with the film *Bambi*, which spread many false ideas about nature, including how deer behave in the presence of a forest fire. According to Roderick Nash, author and professor of environmental studies, *Bambi* "did more to shape American attitudes towards fire in wilderness ecosystems than all the scientific papers ever published on the subject."

Smokey the Bear has also influenced public ideas about forest fires. Since 1945 advertisements featuring Smokey have urged people to prevent forest fires. They have been effective and that's good; no one advocates that people set forests ablaze. However, the advertisements often give the false information that fawns and other wildlife are harmed by wildfires. No doubt this appeal to feelings makes people more careful with fire in the woods, but it also fosters misunderstandings of the role of fire in nature.

Television news directors unwittingly nurture this antifire attitude. Any large object in flames—an apartment house, a warehouse, a forest—yields exciting news film. The news media tend to treat an urban fire and a wilderness fire the same way, as something bad that must be defeated and prevented.

These two kinds of fire are not the same. A goal of the national park system is to conserve native plants and animals and scenic landscapes. In the wilderness of Yellowstone National Park, fire helps achieve that goal. It is not destructive and it does not devastate. It takes life, but also gives it.

Nature does not need to recover or experience a "rebirth" after a forest fire. The Yellowstone ecosystem did not die. It was changed by a force as basic as rain and sunshine. The fires alarmed many people, but were just more in a series that has powerfully influenced the life of the Yellowstone area many times before.

They will again, perhaps 250 years from now. And perhaps by then, we will better understand and appreciate the role of fire in the forest.

GRIZZLY BEAR
(6–7 ft. long)

FURTHER READING AND SOURCES

Carey, Alan and Sandy. *Yellowstone's Red Summer*. Flagstaff, AZ: Northland Publications, 1989.

Christensen, Norman, et al. "Interpreting the Yellowstone Fires of 1988." *Bioscience*, November 1989, pp. 678–685.

Crandall, Hugh. *Yellowstone: The Story Behind the Scenery*. Las Vegas, NV: KC Publications, 1977.

de Golia, Jack. *Fire: The Story Behind a Force of Nature*. Las Vegas, NV: KC Publications, 1989.

Despain, Don. *Yellowstone Vegetation*. Boulder, CO: Roberts Rinehart, Inc., 1990.

Jeffrey, David. "Yellowstone: The Great Fires of 1988." *National Geographic*, February 1989, pp. 255–273.

Knight, Dennis, and Linda Wallace. "The Yellowstone Fires: Issues in Landscape Ecology." *Bioscience*, November 1989, pp. 700–706.

Lauber, Patricia. *Summer of Fire: Yellowstone 1988*. New York: Orchard Books, 1991.

Lewin, Roger. "Ecologists' Opportunity in Yellowstone's Blaze." *Science*, September 13, 1988, pp. 1762–1763.

Patent, Dorothy Hinshaw. *Yellowstone Fires: Flames and Rebirth*. New York: Holiday House, 1990.

Pringle, Laurence. *Natural Fire: Its Ecology in Forests*. New York: William Morrow and Co., 1979.

Robinson, Sandra C. and George B. *Yellowstone in Pictures: The Continuing Story*. Las Vegas, NV: KC Publications, 1990.

Romme, William, and Don Despain. "The Long History of Fire in the Greater Yellowstone Ecosystem." *Western Wildlands*, Summer 1989, pp. 10–17.

———."The Yellowstone Fires." *Scientific American*, November 1989, pp. 37–46.

Singer, Francis, and Paul Schullery. "Yellowstone Wildlife: Populations in Process." *Western Wildlands*, Summer 1989, pp. 18–22.

Staff of the *Billings Gazette*. *Yellowstone on Fire!* Billings, MT: The Billings Gazette, 1989.

Varley, John. "Lessons from the Yellowstone Fires: Do You Trust Talking Animals?" *Transactions of the 55th North American Wildlife and Natural Resources Conference*. Washington, DC: Wildlife Management Institute, 1990.

Wildland Fire in the Northern Rockies (poster). Washington, DC: National Park Service, 1989.

Wuerthner, George. *Yellowstone and the Fires of Change*. Salt Lake City, UT: Haggis House, 1988.